I0829587

CHINYERE

By Joy Ufomadu

Illustrated by Marvin Hollman

ISBN 978-0-9790022-9-8

Chinyere was so excited to be in middle school and even more excited that she was finally a preteen. "Should I wear the brown headband or the black one?" she asked her sister with excitement in her eyes. "The brown one will be perfect for your outfit," her sister replied.

She had planned her First Day of Middle School outfit for the entire summer. Each time that Momma went to the store, there was just one more thing that Chinyere wanted her to pick up.

The day had finally come, and she would finally be in middle school. "Goodbye and God bless you," Daddy said as Chinyere opened the car door and hurried out to line up with her classmates. As everyone got their schedules, she began to feel her heart beat with a nervous excitement. When Chinyere found her class, she was so excited to see that her friends were in the same homeroom as her.

Chinyere found a seat in Mr. Carey's homeroom class. Mr. Carey called the names on his list and, just like in her classes in elementary school, Chinyere's last name was at the bottom of the list. When Mr. Carey finally said her name, she heard a sound that she was not expecting. Snickers.

When she told Mr. Carey the correct way to say her name, the laughter got even louder. Chinyere's classmates were laughing at her name. Her face became warm and her heart began to beat even faster. She just could not believe that people were laughing at her name!

Chinyere had always known that she was different, but she never thought it was a bad thing—until now.

Class after class, period after period, Chinyere heard that same strange sound after her teachers tried to pronounce her name.
By the last period, she was determined to make sure it did not happen ever again.

"Good afternoon. How was your day?" Momma asked as Chinyere got in the car.

"It was good," Chinyere stated in a softer and less excited tone than the one she had that morning.

When Chinyere got home, she decided that she was never going to have this name problem again! She took out her diary, began to brainstorm, and came up with a solution. She was going to go by a simple nickname, like Re-re or Ce-ce.
Then, she decided that she was changing her name completely to something that she thought would be more normal. She didn't have it figured out by dinner time, but she was determined to have a new name by morning.

At the dinner table, Chinyere decided to inform her family of her decision. Her brothers and sister sat eagerly waiting to hear what their parents would say.

"Eh?" Momma questioned in disbelief.

"Come on, stop that nonsense! Haven't we taught you better than that?" Daddy added.

"Chinyere, your name means God's gift!" Momma shouted.

"They don't know that! All they hear is this weird, funny name that doesn't sound like anyone else's," Chinyere replied.

"And what of your last name?" Momma asked.
"Well, I haven't thought about that. But I can just make up something easy," Chinyere said with a nervous smile.
"Easy?" Momma asked in shock.

"Chinyere, you are an Ufomadu. Don't you remember what that means?" Daddy asked her, excited to tell the story again.
"It means, we are still here. Our people are still around!" Daddy exclaimed with a smile.
"Around?" Chinyere asked with a confused look.
"Your great-grandfather chose that name to let everyone know that no matter what, we will always be here, powerful, strong, and united!" Daddy said.

"If he can choose a name, then why can't I?" Chinyere sincerely asked.

"Are you paying attention to what your daddy is saying, Chinyere? If you choose a name that shows how strong, beautiful, and bright you are, we may think about letting you change it. We cannot allow you to change your name because other people cannot understand the beauty in it," Momma said with a warm tone.

"Y'all don't understand and you have never been different!" Chinyere shouted with tears in her eyes.

"We are all different, don't me and your daddy have an accent?" Momma said.

"It's not the same and you know it," Chinyere replied.

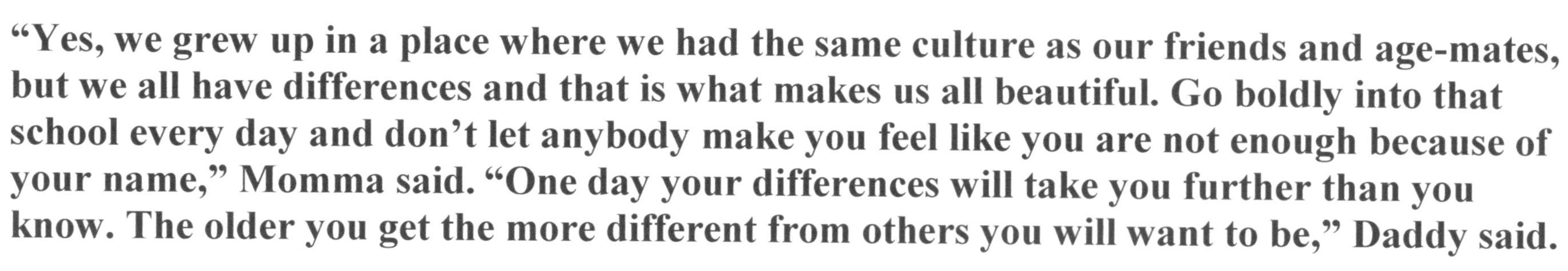

"Yes, we grew up in a place where we had the same culture as our friends and age-mates, but we all have differences and that is what makes us all beautiful. Go boldly into that school every day and don't let anybody make you feel like you are not enough because of your name," Momma said. "One day your differences will take you further than you know. The older you get the more different from others you will want to be," Daddy said.

Chinyere felt a lot better after talking to her parents. She was finally ready to tackle Day 2 of middle school.

"Good night, God bless you," Chinyere said to Momma as her mother peeked in her room that night to make sure that she was okay.

"Good night, God bless you. Don't forget that no matter what anybody tries to say tomorrow or any day, your name is Chinyere! You are my sister's namesake," Momma said proudly.

"Yes ma'am," Chinyere replied with a smile.

"Don't you let there be a morning that you forget to say 'My name is Chinyere and I am beautiful,'" Chinyere's mother instructed before closing her room door.

Chinyere went to school the next feeling very confident and proud of her name. She even wore an ankara print scarf that day to show pride in her African culture.
"I am beautiful, and my name is Chinyere Ufomadu," she said to herself before she walked into school that day and all of the rest of her days in middle school.

Have you ever felt ashamed of the things that make you different from others? Think about all of the things that make you unique and list why they are positive!

Chinyere wore her Ankara print scarf to school to celebrate her uniqueness. Write down things that you can do to celebrate yours!

9 780979 002298